ALWAYS WONDER.
ALWAYS WANDER.

This ... is Sebastian. Sebastian Scouts.
And seemingly ordinary by any account.

Except that he's not; he's anything but.
Like all Scouts before him, he adventures about.

From near to far and far to near,
Scouts have explored, invented, pioneered.

Why his great grandfather, Sir Spencer Scouts,
Invented a whale translator his legacy touts.

Sir Spencer Scouts

And grandfather Samuel, an explorer by trade,
Discovered 32 new species,
which after him 12 were named.

Shrugging Sammy
"No Strong Opinions"

Stupendous Sam
"Really quite tall indeed"

Adolescent Ameul
"You don't get it"

Striped Samuel
"Proud of his stripes"

Smart Hop Sam
"Always looks first"

Soaring Sammy
"Beat the odds to fly!"

Singing Samuel

"The most lovely singing voice"

And Shepard, his father, astronaut engineer,
Discovered new constellations as a space pioneer.

And Sebastian's no different; he is just the same.
Like those before him,
he will honor the Scouts name.

With Maverick and Agnes and Pippa and Finn,

12

PEOPLES REPUBLIC
28 AUG
OF AWESOME

ISLAND OF WIN
17 SEP 202

WE ARE THE ADVENTURERS,
PIONEERS, EXPLORERS AND
INVENTORS OF THE WORLD
WE WANT TO LIVE IN

Finn

Signature of Adventurer

UNITED ADVENTURERS CLUB

CLUB PASS
Photo

Full Name
Finn

Code Name
Big Flipper

Home Country
Falkland Islands

Date of Birth
09 July 2013

Home Town
Stanley

Date of Issue
21 AUG 2012

Adventurer Specialty
Comedy
Marine Life

Animal
Gentoo Penguin

Authority
Scouts Guild
Department of Explorati

UAC

CLUB PASS
Photo

Full Name
Agnes

Code Name
Quick Draw

Home Country
China

Date of Birth
16 April 2010

Home Town
Lincang

Date of Issue
21 Ju

Adventurer Specialty
Drawing
History

Animal
Asian Elephant

Authority
Scouts Guild
Department

WE ARE
PIONEERS, EXPLORERS
INVENTORS OF THE WORLD
WE WANT TO LIVE IN

Pippa

Signature of Adventurer

UNITED ADVENTURERS CLUB

CLUB PASS
Photo

Full Name
Pippa

Code Name
Teach

Home Country
Kenya

Date of Birth
05 March 2009

Home Town
Mombasa

Date of Issue
18 September 2013

Adventurer Specialty
Jungles
Sprinting

Animal
Leopard

Authority
Scouts Guild
Department of Exploration

UAC

WE ARE
PIONEER
INVENTO
WE W

Mave

Signature o

UNITED AD

CLUB PASS
Photo

Full Name
Maverick

Code Name
Pappa Bear

Home Country
United States of America

Date of Birth
19 November 2010

Home Town
Yellowstone

Date of Issue
09 February 2014

Adventurer Specialty
Courage
Forests

Animal
Brown Bear

Authority
Scouts Guild
Department of Exploration

UAC

UNITED ADVENTURERS
CLUB

UNITED ADVENTURERS CLUB

Every day's an adventure waiting to begin.

Their newest adventure - just wait, take a seat -
Is besting a world record that's NEVER been beat!

Someone long ago, someone far away,
Traveled all 7 Wonders in just under 3 days!

The World Wonders Crew - Adventure Award Ceremony

So with friends all in tow and trip plotted out,
They set course to the first stop on the mapped route.

Taking photos of each place they planned to go,
First Chichen Itza, "¡Hola Mexico!"

Next, Christ the Redeemer overlooking Brazil.
Then to Peru's Machu Picchu - oh what a thrill!

But there's not a second to spare; no time to waste.
If they want to break the record,
they'd better make haste!

The Colosseum in Rome was next on the list,
and the rock walls of Jordan were not to be missed!

But there's no time to wander; no time to explore.
The race is nearly done
but with still two stops more.

In India they marveled at the grand Taj Mahal.

And then quickly to China to scale the Great Wall.

With all places visited
and stopwatch recorded,

They wished, hoped and prayed
for efforts rewarded.

With time to spare for the fearless Scouts crew,
They'd broken the record by not one day but two!

SUPER KID JOURNAL

Your trusted source for all kid adventurer, explorer, inventor and pioneer news

Sebastian Scouts' Squad Scores!

It's Official - Judges Report Incredible Victory Yesterday Afternoon

"I couldn't have done it without my friends," Scouts said.

They shouted! They cheered!
They high-fived each other.
Oh what an adventure. Now time for another!